LITTLE GRAY ONE

by Jan Wahl · pictures by Frané Lessac

TAMBOURINE BOOKS · NEW YORK

Text copyright © 1993 by Jan Wahl
Illustrations copyright © 1993 by Frané Lessac

All rights reserved. No part of this book may be reproduced or
utilized in any form or by any means, electronic or mechanical,
including photocopying, recording, or by any information storage
or retrieval system, without permission in writing from the
Publisher. Inquiries should be addressed to
Tambourine Books, a division of William Morrow & Company, Inc.,
1350 Avenue of the Americas, New York, New York 10019.
The illustrations were painted in gouache on paper.
Printed in the United States of America.

Library of Congress Cataloging in Publication Data

Wahl, Jan. Little Gray One/by Jan Wahl;
illustrated by Frané Lessac.—1st ed. p. cm.
Summary: Mother Elephant teaches her child to forage for food,
bathe in the water, and play where it is safe.
1. Elephants—Juvenile fiction. [1. Elephants—Fiction.]
I. Lessac, Frané, ill. II. Title.
PZ10.3.W1295Li 1993 [E]—dc20 92-33776 CIP AC
ISBN 0-688-12037-7.—ISBN 0-688-12038-5 (lib. bdg.)
1 3 5 7 9 10 8 6 4 2
FIRST EDITION

For Hannah Casselton and her parents
J.W.

For Estelle, Jeannie, and Carol
F.L.

The sun is rising,
a huge pink ball of light.
It is Elephant morning.

Storks fly up, up
and so do cranes.
This is where Little Gray One lives.

This is where lions stand in tall grass.
This is where quick cheetahs run
with beautiful gazelles.
This is the place of the water hole.

"Wake up, Little Gray One,"
says Mother Elephant.
He rubs sleep from his eyes.
"What do we do today?" he asks.

She answers by yanking up a black plum tree.
"This is how to pick the very best
leaves and fruit," she says.
"A plum for you.
A plum for me."

Softly, Mother Elephant touches his trunk.
"I love you, Little Gray One."
She pushes him toward the water hole.

"First, dip in the water.
Now roll in the dust.
It is cooling.
A bath for you, a bath for me."
They become the color of sweet red earth.

Little Gray One is frisky
and joins a herd.
Wildebeest hoofs fly.
They leap and buck, spin and kick.
"Look, look! I am a wildebeest!"

"No you are not," says his mother.
"You are an elephant."
She grabs his tail in her trunk,
steering him away.

"I am hungry,"
whimpers Little Gray One.
He watches a zebra nibbling weeds.

His mother tugs at grass
and shakes off dirt.
"I want berries," he says.

"Wait. They are not ripe,"
she says and plucks pumpkins,
juicy and round.
"One for you. One for me."
He chews, flicking his tail.

They walk together.
Buzzards wheel overhead.
The day grows hot.

"Step under this fig tree,"
says Mother Elephant.
A giraffe pays no attention to them.

"My back is itchy," says Little Gray One.
"Mine too," says Mother Elephant.
"Rub against an anthill.
Isn't it good?
One for you. One for me."

Brown monkeys climb down baobab trees
to hop on Little Gray One's back.
He squeals and races
with ears flapping.

The monkeys want to cross a wide marsh.
He gets stuck!
Monkeys chatter noisily.

Somehow, his mother pulls him loose.
"You are not ready
to take monkeys riding," she says.

A long cobra stretches on the ground.
Mother Elephant shouts
and shakes her head to chase it away.
"You are safe. I am always near,"
she whispers.

"I am safe but thirsty," he sighs.
With strong tusks and forefeet
she digs two holes.

Out of nowhere spring puddles.
"One for you
and one for me."

Little Gray One sees an acacia tree.
"I am hungry," he says.
"Be careful for thorns,"
his mother tells him.

It is dusk.
Pelicans wade in the river,
far from crocodiles.
Night is coming soon.

Old Ancient One sways
at the water's edge.
His tusks are yellow and broken.
He trumpets to the other elephants.

From across the plain, down the valley,
from everywhere, elephants gather.
They do a slow and
shuffling dance.

Mother Elephant curls her trunk
with Little Gray One's.
He leans against her.

Quietly, Mother Elephant says,
"There is much to learn, child."
He rubs his eyes
and yawns.

"I learned a lot today," he says.
She croons and cuddles him
in the twilight.
"Sleep in peace, Little Gray One."

And the moon rays shine down to keep them warm.